This
MOUSE ◨ WORKS
Classics Collection Storybook

belongs to

_____

DISNEY's Bambi

MOUSE WORKS

Also available in Spanish

© 1989, 1996 Disney Enterprises, Inc.
The edition containing the full text of *Bambi, A Life in the Woods*
by Felix Salten is published by Simon & Schuster.
Printed in the United States of America
ISBN: 1-57082-403-7
3 5 7 9 10 8 6 4

As the night faded into the dawn, the creatures of the forest awoke to find the long winter was over. Baby birds chirped, hungry for their breakfast of berries. Mice scurried through the tall blades of grass, bathing in the drops of dew. Squirrels and chipmunks enjoyed nuts and acorns in their treetop homes. Everyone was busy working and playing in the golden sunshine of spring's first day.

3

But a wonderful surprise soon stopped all the activity. Bluebirds soared through the skies chirping the news and all the animals followed them—all except the sleepy old owl who had settled in for his nap.

"Wake up, Friend Owl!" shouted a little rabbit named Thumper. He thumped his hind leg against the bark with excitement. "It's happened! A new prince is born!"

All the animals gathered in a sunlit thicket where a mama deer and her baby lay.

"Well, this is quite an occasion," said the owl. "You are to be congratulated."

"Yes, congratulations!" echoed the animals.

"We have company," the doe said, tenderly nuzzling the fawn with her nose. The baby blinked his big brown eyes and perked his ears up.

"Hello, little prince!" the animals called.

The little prince tried to stand and greet his visitors, pulling himself up on his long, thin legs. But he teetered and tottered and flopped right back down.

"Kinda wobbly, isn't he?" Thumper giggled, hopping close to the fawn for a better look. "Whatcha gonna call 'im?"

The doe looked lovingly at her baby, now snuggled at her side. "I think I'll call him Bambi."

Several dawns came and went in the forest, and Bambi grew bigger and stronger.

"Walking already!" exclaimed a squirrel as the fawn tried his hardest to prance proudly behind his mother on the leafy path.

"Good morning, young prince!" called the mother possum.

"Good morning, young prince!" her three babies repeated.

Bambi turned his head upside down to greet them. There were so many wonderful things to find in the forest! Every new day was filled with surprises, and Bambi could hardly wait to see what would happen next.

"Good morning!" called a mole before ducking back down his hole and scurrying away.

Bambi followed the burrowed trail, trying to catch a glimpse of the dark, furry creature. But his legs weren't quite steady enough yet to run, and he tripped over a tall reed and landed with a loud thump on the ground.

"Did the young prince fall down?" asked Thumper.
He and his brother and sister bunnies gathered
around Bambi to cheer him on.

"Come on!" they urged. "Get up! Try again!"
Bambi struggled to pull himself up. He wasn't
about to miss any of the fun! He wobbled and
wiggled as the bunnies giggled.

The bunnies showed Bambi so many new things. "Those are birds," Thumper explained, as a flock of baby bluebirds nibbled berries on a branch.

"Burr!" Bambi repeated.

"Say bird!" Thumper corrected, wiggling his pink nose. "Bur-duh."

"Bird!" Bambi shouted, and the birds scattered into the air.

"Bird!" Bambi called out when a yellow butterfly landed on his tail.

"That's not a bird." Thumper laughed at his friend. "That's a butterfly!"

The butterfly flew off into a patch of brightly colored flowers, and Bambi followed.

"Butterfly," Bambi said, poking his nose into the beautiful blooms.

"No, Bambi." Thumper chuckled again. "That's a flower."

When Bambi bent over to sniff the sweetly scented blossoms again, he found himself nose to nose with another furry friend.

"Flower," he announced proudly.

Thumper rolled on the ground with laughter. "No, no, no," he said. "That's not a flower! He's a little—"

The shy little skunk spoke softly. "Aw, that's all right," he said. "Gosh, he can call me a flower if he wants to."

Thumper and Bambi continued to play until a sudden clap of thunder sent the little bunny scurrying.

"I think I better go home now," Thumper called as he raced back into the woods for cover. Bambi returned to his warm, dry thicket just as lightning began to crackle across the black sky.

Bambi nestled close to his mother for a nap, but the sound of the rain falling in soft drip-drops on the leaves kept him awake. The squirrel in the tree wrapped himself in his big furry tail. The mama bird covered her babies with her big wings, and a tiny mouse ducked beneath a toadstool umbrella. Soon all the animals—even Bambi— were lulled to sleep by the gentle pitter-patter.

Bambi learned that the April showers brought beautiful flowers to the meadow. His mother took him there one day, on a long, winding trail past the sparkling waterfall.

"Why haven't I been to the meadow before?" he asked her.

"You weren't big enough," she said, hushing him as they reached the edge of the forest. "We're almost there."

In the distance, Bambi saw the meadow. It was lush and green and dotted with clover and blossoms. He darted out ahead, eager to romp in the wide-open space—but his mother leaped in front of him.

"You must never rush out on the meadow!" she scolded. "There might be danger!"

Bambi's mother went first, moving silently and looking from side to side. When she was sure it was safe, she called for Bambi to join her. The meadow didn't seem like a scary place, Bambi thought, scampering beside his mother—it seemed like fun!

"Whatcha eatin'?" Bambi called to Thumper. He was sitting in a patch of purple flowers, happily munching.

"Eat the flowers," the bunny advised, "not that green stuff!"

Bambi nodded and plunged into a pile of clover. His nose met something cold and clammy. It was a frog—and he was not at all happy with Bambi nosing around in his hiding place.

"Watch out!" the frog croaked, jumping high into the air.

Bambi followed the frog to a shimmering pond. He watched as it hopped from rock to rock, then disappeared beneath the shiny, rippled surface with a splash. Bambi bent his face close to the water and stared at his reflection. He saw a fawn that looked exactly like him.

But as Bambi watched, there were suddenly two reflections in the water—and one was definitely not him! It smiled and laughed and fluttered its eyelashes.

It was another baby deer—a girl—and she teased and tickled him, until Bambi nervously ran behind his mother's legs.

"That's little Faline," his mother explained. "Go on," she nudged him. "Say hello."

Bambi closed his eyes and gulped. "Hello," he said as Faline giggled. She started another game of tag—and Bambi was "it"!

"What kind of trick is she up to this time?"
Bambi wondered.

Suddenly, Faline pounced and Bambi stumbled
backwards, landing with a loud splash in the pond.
She poked her head through the reeds and licked
his face playfully. Bambi squirmed and took off after
her, butting her with his head. Before long, the two
were best friends.

Bambi and Faline stopped playing when they heard hooves thundering in the distance. A herd of stags galloped by them onto the meadow. Then another stag—the biggest one of all—stopped and looked straight at Bambi. Bambi lowered his eyes, but he could still feel the great stag's majestic gaze.

"Why was everyone still when he came on the meadow?" Bambi asked, drawing close to his mother.

"Everyone respects him," she whispered. "He is very brave and very wise. He is the Great Prince of the Forest." He was also Bambi's father.

The silence was shattered by a loud blast. Bambi
thought it sounded like a clap of thunder. But it was a
gunshot—Man was in the forest.

All the animals stampeded, heading for the safety of
the dark, dense trees and shrubs.

"Mother, where are you?" Bambi shrieked, frantically
trying to find her.

"Bambi! Bambi!" he heard her cry. "Hurry!"

The Great Prince guided him to his mother and their
thicket. Once again, they were safe and sound.

Time passed swiftly in the forest, and Bambi woke one morning to find the wind had turned cold and the whole world was covered in a soft white blanket.

"It's snow," Bambi's mother told him. "It means winter has come."

Bambi tested the snow under his hooves. It was wet and cold, but he liked the way it crunched beneath his steps and left tracks behind him.

Thumper called to his friend from a frozen pond. "Watch what I can do!" the bunny said, spinning and swirling expertly across the ice. "Come on—it's all right! The water's stiff."

Bambi stood for a moment, marveling at the glittering pond.

"Yippee!" he yelled, leaping into the air. He landed on all fours on the ice—Thumper had forgotten to warn him how slippery it was! His front legs went one way, his back legs went the other way, and he belly-flopped with a hard thud.

Thumper skated over to him. "Some fun, huh, Bambi?"

Thumper tried to teach Bambi how to skate, pushing his back legs up, then pulling his front legs straight. But instead, the deer got all tangled up.

"Ya gotta watch both ends at the same time!" the bunny advised, helping his friend unwind. With a push from Thumper, Bambi was finally gliding across the ice—but where were the brakes?

The pair landed in a snowbank by a cave. Inside, Flower was snoring. Thumper thumped hello.

"Wake up, Flower!" called Bambi. But the little skunk just yawned and stretched.

"Is it spring yet?" he asked.

"Nope, winter's just starting," Bambi replied, eager for his friend to join in the fun.

"All of us flowers sleep in the winter," Flower said, tucking himself under his tail. "Good night."

Winter was fun at first, but after a while, Bambi longed for the warm spring days that had brought with them delicious grass and flowers.

"I'm hungry, Mother," Bambi said, as they pawed the ground, searching for a few blades of grass buried beneath the snow. When they could find none, they nibbled tree bark, but Bambi missed the sweet blossoms he had snacked on in the meadow.

"Winter seems long, but it won't last forever," his mother assured him.

One day, they found a small patch of grass pushing up through the snow. To Bambi, it was a feast! He nibbled hungrily, but noticed his mother wasn't eating. She had lifted her head to listen.

In the distance, a gun shot rang out. Bambi's eyes widened in fear—he knew what that horrible sound meant. Man was in the forest again.

"Quick, run for the thicket, Bambi!" his mother instructed. "Don't look back!"

Bambi ran and ran, his heart pounding as his hooves kicked up snow behind him.

"Faster!" he heard his mother call. "Keep running!"

All he could think of was reaching the thicket and being safe and warm once again. He heard a second shot just as he reached his home.

"Mother!" Bambi screamed into the snowy woods. "Mother, where are you?"

He frantically searched between the towering trees, but she was nowhere in sight. He listened hard for her voice calling him, but heard only the soft, falling flakes and the wind whistling through the barren branches. At that moment, Bambi realized he was alone.

Bambi was crying when he sensed a tall shadow standing over him. It was the Great Prince.

"Your mother," the stag said softly, "can't be with you anymore. Man has taken her away."

Bambi lowered his head sadly and swallowed back his tears.

"Come, my son," the stag told him.

Bambi looked sadly back at the thicket one last time. Then he followed the Great Prince into the forest.

Time flew quickly, and the long winter was at last over. Once again, the forest came alive. The flowers bloomed, the ground sprouted greenery, and the birds twittered excitedly in the trees. Even Flower awakened from his nap!

The spring brought with it many changes. Bambi was now a handsome young buck with antlers, and Thumper was a full-grown rabbit.

"Well, well—look how you've grown!" said Friend Owl to the three friends. "It won't be long now before you're twitterpated!"

Bambi, Flower, and Thumper looked at each other, puzzled.

"Nearly everybody gets twitterpated in the springtime," the owl explained. "You get weak in the knees. Your head starts to whirl. Before you know it, you're knocked for a loop!"

"Well, it's not gonna happen to me," declared Thumper.

"Me, neither!" agreed Bambi.

But it was too late for Flower. He met a pretty skunk and fell for her. Shrugging, he waved good-bye to his friends.

"Huh!" Thumper sniffed, disgusted by his friend's behavior. "Twitterpated!"

Thumper was the next one to be struck by the mysterious condition Owl had warned them about. "La, la, la," sang a beautiful bunny. She waved hello with her ear and rubbed noses with him. Thumper's foot began thumping.

Bambi still didn't quite understand what twitterpated was until he saw a familiar reflection in the water as he was drinking from the pond.

"Hello, Bambi!" said a sweet female voice. Startled, Bambi stumbled back, his antlers getting stuck in a branch of blossoms.

"Don't you remember me? I'm Faline," the doe giggled and licked his face.

Bambi felt suddenly dizzy, as if he were light as a feather. This, he thought, must be what Owl meant!

Bambi and Faline frolicked together in the meadow
just as they had done last summer. He had never been
so happy! He closed his eyes, dreamily, and pictured
them romping through the clouds.

But the dream faded quickly when a stag appeared and challenged him for Faline.

The two deer locked antlers, tossing each other against the hard ground. Bambi fought fiercely, pushing the stag to the edge of a cliff.

"Bambi!" Faline cried out in alarm.

Bambi butted the stag with all his might, sending him rolling down the hill into the river below. The stag limped off into the forest, leaving Bambi and Faline to be together.

From that day on, Bambi and Faline were always at each other's side. They galloped together through the moonlit meadow as fireflies and fallen blossoms swirled in the air. They made their home in the thicket and lived happily, until one morning, Bambi sensed danger in the forest.

"It's Man," the Great Prince told him. "There are many this time." The smell of a smoking campfire wafted through the air. "We must go deep into the forest."

Fear spread through the forest as crows shouted a warning. "Be calm! Don't get excited!" urged a pheasant, but the animals panicked. Man was coming!

Thumper gathered his young into hiding in their burrow, and Flower and his family went underground. The beavers dove underwater, and the squirrels climbed high into the treetops, as the rest of the animals raced deeper and deeper into the forest.

"Bambi! Bambi!" Faline cried in terror. She could hear the sounds of Man's angry dogs coming nearer. She scrambled up steep slopes, just as a pack of snarling hounds burst out of the bushes behind her. Barking and biting, they chased her up the rocky cliff, snapping at her heels. She was trapped!

Just then, the dogs turned to attack something else. Bambi was fighting them off so Faline could flee! As he charged with his sharp antlers, Faline bounded up the cliff to safety.

Bambi had fought off the pack of dogs, but he couldn't escape Man's rifle. A shot rang out, and Bambi fell. He tried his hardest, but he could not get up.

He raised his head weakly to see smoke pouring through the trees and animals running in fear.

"You must get up!" It was the voice of his father, the Great Prince, at his side. "Get up!"

Bambi tried again and fell back down.

Bambi staggered to his feet and began to run. Smoke filled the air, and he could feel the heat of the fire on his coat. The red flames spread like fingers over the forest. They climbed up trees and over bushes, surrounding the once beautiful forest in an eerie orange glow.

"Follow me," the Great Prince said. "We'll be safe in the river."

The whole forest was ablaze, and the smoke made it hard for Bambi to breathe, but his father forced him on. When they reached the river, they swam with all their might toward the falls. With the fire behind them, they would have to jump.

Both Bambi and the Great Prince leaped high in the air, disappearing down the falls just as a flaming tree crashed inches behind them.

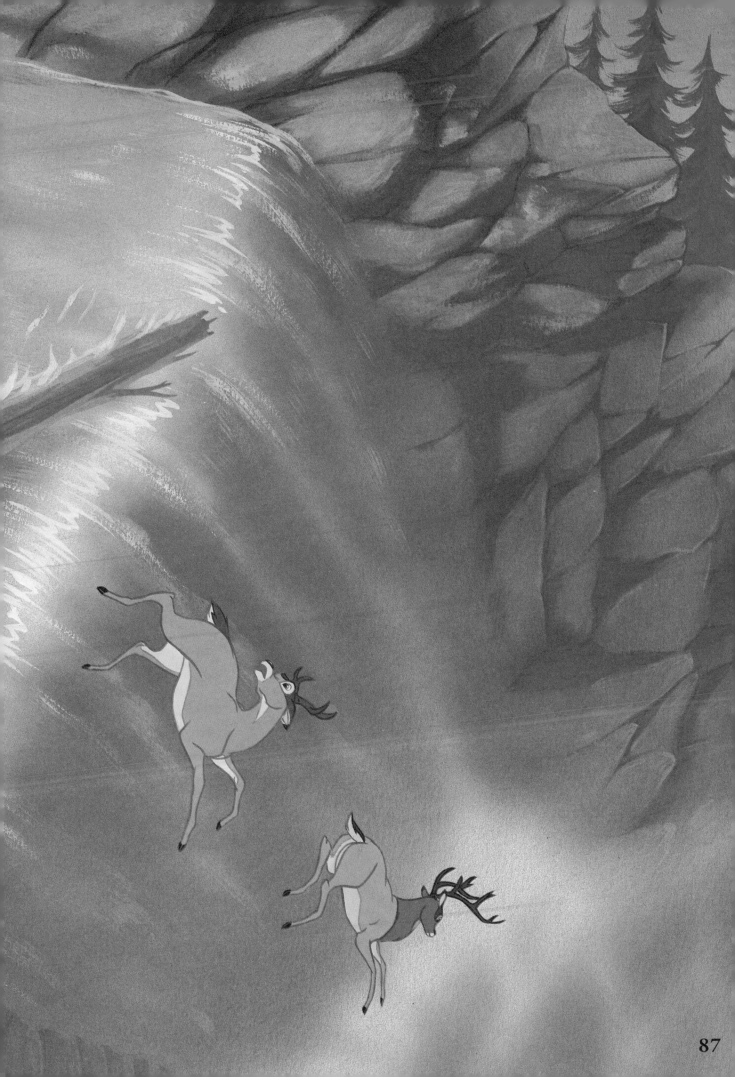

When they reached an island in the river, Faline was waiting for Bambi. She gently licked his wounded shoulder. They watched that night as fire destroyed their forest home—all the towering trees and delicate blossoms were now blackened. But tomorrow, they knew, when the fire was out and Man was gone, the animals would bravely rebuild their homes.

The warm summer months gave way to crisp autumn. Then came cold, white winter. But before long, it was once again spring and time to start anew.

"Wake up, Friend Owl!" Thumper and his four baby bunnies all thumped on a hollow log.

"What now?" groaned the grumpy old owl. The squirrels and pheasants, quail and chipmunks, raccoons and rabbits were all racing for a familiar thicket.

"Hurry up!" called Flower, his own baby skunk trailing behind him.

"Well, sir, I don't believe I've ever seen a more likely lookin' pair of fawns!" the owl said, nodding his head. "Prince Bambi ought to be mighty proud."

Prince Bambi was proud as he stood with his father on a hill overlooking the thicket where Faline lay with her new fawns. Bambi, the new Prince of the Forest, would teach them the ways of the world that he had learned himself a long, long time ago.

Though year after year had passed in the forest, a new adventure was just beginning for Bambi and his young family.

The proud parents and their fawns were starting out on a new journey together. And life in the forest would never be the same again!